Gertrude Health

Rhymes and jingles for a good child

Gertrude Health

Rhymes and jingles for a good child

ISBN/EAN: 9783337273903

Printed in Europe, USA, Canada, Australia, Japan

Cover: Foto ©Andreas Hilbeck / pixelio.de

More available books at **www.hansebooks.com**

For A Good Child

GERTRUDE E. HEATH.

THE EDITOR PUBLISHING CO.,
CINCINNATI, O.
1897.

TO

EIGHT COUSINS.

CONTENTS.

5

RHYMES AND JINGLES.

CHRISTMAS MORN.

CHRISTMAS morn, fair Christmas morn,
  In His beauty Christ was born!
Years ago, ah! years ago!
  Pure as lilies in the snow
Came the Christ-child, pure and loving,
  All the Father's kindness proving.
Fair and sweet, O fair and sweet!
  Kiss the tiny hands and feet!
Toward the Shepherd of His sheep
  Love can never be too deep!

Ring the bells, ah! ring the bells!
  Tell it to the glades and dells!
How to-day—glad to-day'—
  Christ is worshipped far away.
Born in humble, lonely manger,
  Came a King e'er holier, stranger?
Bow your heads, O bow your heads!
  Far too bright the light He sheds.
Lay your offerings—it is meet—
  Lowly at the Christ-child's feet!

7

Then rejoice! O then rejoice!
  With a happy heart and voice.
Let no tears, O let no tears!
  Dim the brightest of our years.
Under earth the roots are growing
  Buds for other summer's blowing.
Fair and sweet, O fair and sweet!
  Kiss the tiny hands and feet!
Toward the Shepherd of His sheep
  Love can never be too deep!

WAKE.

Wake up, grasses!
   Wake up, clover!
See! the cold is
   Almost over!

Here is April.
   See! she's weeping!
All her babes so
   Soundly sleeping!

Wake up, posies!
   April's going!
Comes the May-time,
   Time of blowing!

Wake up, grasses!
   Wake up, clover!
See! the cold is
   Almost over!

EASTER.

UNDER their blankets of snow
    The flowers were lying asleep:
And every ice-bound brook
    Lay locked in a slumber deep.
The Robin away in the South
    Talked of his Northern home,
And carolled merrily forth:
    "Wait till the summer come!"
Gray clouds went over the sky,
    But behind them shone the Sun:
He was only waiting his time
    Till the Winter's work was done.

The flowers were waked in their beds
    By the sound of the falling rain;
They knew what the summons meant—
    They were called to the world again!
The brooks, released from their bonds,
    Went merrily bounding along
Over the moss-grown stones
    To the tune of the Robin's song.
For the Robin, too, came back
    To his home in the old pine tree,
And he waked the woods with his song,
    And the sound of his melody.

And the dainty buds bloomed out.
    And the leaves came back to the trees.
All for the April sun.
    And the kiss of the Western breeze.
O typical life of the flowers,
    Crushed under the foot as we tread!
So Christ awoke in a far-off land
    From the silent sleep of the dead.
There are holy songs in the air.
    Hark! Christ is arisen to-day,
For His angels came to the grave,
    And they rolled the stone away!

THE ROSE FAIRY.

ONCE upon a time there lived a Fairy
　Down in the heart of a sweet wild rose,
And all that she wore was the quaintest costume,
　A queer little suit of calico clothes.

Never she cared if the warm rains wet her;
　Loud she laughed in her dainty nest!
What care I for the rain-drop's kisses,
　Down in the heart of the wild rose's breast?

Once upon a time the wild rose withered,
　All in the heat of a summer's day!
Where went then our queer little Fairy?
　Opened her wings and far she flew away!

Only to-day I was picking roses,
　What did I find in a rosebud snug?
Fast asleep from her summer's travels,
　A dear little, queer little Lady-bug!

STRAWBERRY'S SURPRISE.

SWEET little Strawberry Blossom
   Sat nodding in the sun:
She said: "When breezes dance me,
   O what delicious fun!"
Just then a merry Zephyr,
   Who was gaily rushing by,
Took Blossom's white hat with him,
   Said Strawberry Blossom, "Why?"

The warm Sun smiling brightly
   Kissed Berry's drooping head:
She hung it lower, lower,
   And blushed a rosy red.
A little brown-cheeked urchin
   Espied her bending low,
And bore her home to mamma,
   Said Ripe-red Berry, "Oh!"

THE FIRST MAYFLOWER.

Down under her leaflets,
  Snug hidden away,
A little May maiden
  A-sleeping there lay.

Green grew her leaflets
  In spite of the cold,
And deep grew her brown roots
  A-down in the mold.

Rain-drop came knocking;
  Wake up, little flower!
The robin's are calling,
  O wait not an hour!

The little May-blossom
  Peeped out at the sky,
And laughed at the clouds
  That went scurrying by.

And when a breeze kissed her,
  A-flush was her face;
And little May-blossom
  Was first in her place.

14

JOE.

WE had planned some grand surprises,
    Hugh and I,
As the tearful days of April
    Glided by ;
We had fashioned quaint May-baskets,
    Great and small,
And with brown nuts from the garret
    Filled them all.
But the greatest of our secrets
    No one knew,
Save the urchins in the garret,
    I and Hugh.

Down the lane a quaint old cottage
    Stood alone,
Just beyond our orchard's crumbling
    Wall of stone.
Here lived one poor, sad-eyed woman
    And her boy ;
In their home there never entered
    Smallest joy.
Joe, the child, had never joined us
    In our plays ;
We almost forgot him living
    Those bright days.

No one noticed him, poor baby!
    'Round his door
Only dandelions and daisies
    By the score
Raised their bright heads, smiled upon him,
    Kissed his feet:
He returned their love with kisses
    Warm and sweet.
We had seen him kiss them often,
    And we smiled:
He was wiser far than we were,
    Lonely child!

Yes, he loved the flower faces
    Small and bright:
This had led us to our secret
    For May-night.
Hand in hand down through the orchard
    I and Hugh
Went for sweet Arbutus blossoms
    Wet with dew.
There we found them, waxen blossoms
    Pink and white,
Hiding under leafy coverts
    From the light.

Laughingly we bore them homeward
    Through the lane;
Held them up to faces watching
    'Gainst the pane.

But we whispered not our secret;
    And at night
Crept down softly through the orchard
    Out of sight.
Low down bent the apple branches,
    And a breeze
Kissed our foreheads as we hastened laughing
    Through the trees.

"Go!" it whispered; "God be with you!"
    God was there,
Nearer than we ever thought Him
    Anywhere.
Something in the silence awed us,
    Hushed our words,
And we left the orchard quiet
    As its birds.
Hand in hand we reached the cottage;
    At the door
Left our May-blooms; came home faster
    Than before.

This was years ago this May-time;
    Yet I pray
We may ne'er forget the lesson
    Of that day!
For the kindness so late coming
    Found poor Joe
Silent as his daisies sleeping
    'Neath the snow!

And the blossoms we had brought him
Glad and proud,
Lay all scattered and unnoticed
On a shroud!

THE REASON WHY.

To-DAY the first June rose bloomed out,
  Down by the daisies and clover;
All a-tremble, with leaves a-pout,
  Buttercups bending over.

"Sweet, so sweet!" the butterfly said,
  "Rose in your rustic splendor!"
And honey-bees lingered over her head,
  Murmuring love-words tender.

Sweet, little, blushing, wayside Rose,
  Tell me what is the reason
All of your brothers and sisters sleep,
  You are first of the season?

All a-blushing the little Rose said:
  "I know they can not have missed me!
I waked this morning (she hung her head)
  Because a honey-bee kissed me!"

MABEL IN THE MEADOW.

TRIPPING through the meadow grass
    Past the nodding clover,
Goes my little fair-haired lass
    Tripping through the meadow grass!
Robins greet her as they pass—
    Greet her o'er and over,
Tripping through the meadow grass
    Past the nodding clover!

Buttercups and daisies sweet,
    Daisies white and yellow,
Bow beneath her dainty feet—
    Buttercups and daisies sweet;
Bow till root and blossom meet
    In the brown earth mellow,
Buttercups and daisies sweet—
    Daisies white and yellow.

Every blossom bloomed for you,
    Dainty little maiden!
Blue-eyed grasses wet with dew,
    Every blossom bloomed for you;
Clover sweet and meadow rue
    In your basket laden;
Every blossom bloomed for you,
    Dainty little maiden!

WHAT THE DEW-DROP TOLD THE CHILDREN.

Come, my wee ones, gazing wisely
    At my Pansy's purple heart,
I will tell you of my lifetime,
    All the glad and bitter part.
Heaven was once my home, dear children,
    All my friends were Rain-drops bright,
But they left their home and kindred,
    Took the way they knew was right.

But I stayed behind, unwilling;
    In my home preferred to live,
Though I knew your thirsty Planet
    Needed help that I could give.
"Nay," I said to my dear comrades,
    "One wee drop can do no good!"
So they left me, sad and sorry,
    To be happy if I could.

But the hours passed on in sadness;
    Vainly I for gladness sought;
For I missed my former comrades,
    Longed for joy their lives had brought.

Late one morning in the Autumn
  I put on my robe of white,
And no more they called me Rain-drop,
  But the Snowflake, pure and white.

Wearied then was I of Cloud-land;
  So I urged my friends to go
Fill the air with fleecy brightness,
  And to wreathe the earth with snow.
Gladly then each one assented,
  Gaily started on his way,
Floating idly in the ether,
  Laughing in the face of day.

Soon we neared your gloomy Planet.
  Saw the Earth a barren land,
Waiting to be changed to beauty
  By our Artist's master hand.
Sad I gazed upon the Planet;
  Thought that I could do no good,
As I looked o'er lake and river,
  Mountain, hill, and waving wood.

But I spied in one glad moment,
  In your garden, bare and dead,
One wee, modest, little Pansy
  Nodding in her lonely bed.
Glad I sank into her bosom,
  But she shuddered at the cold;
I could feel the chill; it filled me
  With a sadness deep, untold!

Suddenly the snow-clouds breaking
   Let the genial sunlight through,
And my Pansy sweet discovered
   She but held a drop of dew!
Gaily then the Flakes danced 'round her!
   Said with laughter sweet and loud,
" You will find a silver lining,
   Little flower, to every cloud!"

ASTER AND GOLDEN-ROD.

Two plants within the meadow
   Grew upward, side by side,
Nor yet fulfilled their mission
   Until the summer died.

Taller they grew and taller,
   Nor knew each other near
Till Golden-rod leaned over,
   " Wake up! Wake up! my dear!"

Sweet Aster shook her leaflets,
   And ope'd her fringèd eyes,
And gazed at Roddy Golden
   With quaint and pleased surprise.

Then Golden-rod laughed gaily,
   And shook his yellow locks :
"Cold winter soon is coming,
   Put on your warmest frocks!"

But Aster—ah, vain Aster!—
   Was proud as proud could be :
" Dress in a darker color?"
   Said Aster; No, not she!

24

Her dainty purple garments,
    Ah! fair were they to see!
They seemed like snow-drifts tinted
    By sunsets o'er the lea!

Days passed. The two were happy,
    And Golden-rod each week
Bent nearer to his sweetheart,
    Until he touched her cheek!

"Dear heart, you would not listen!
    Look up above your head!
The snows will soon be falling,
    For, darling, Summer's dead!

"We cannot bear the snow-falls;
    Sweet Aster, we must die;
But we will die together,
    I'll never say good-by!"

The flakes of snow, light laughing,
    Came dancing o'er the sod;
Wrapped in one shroud they left them,
    Aster and Golden-rod!

LITTLE WHITE CLOVER.

I HEARD the fickle bee one night
    As merrily he flew over,
Making love with a honeyed lip
    To dainty little White Clover—
" Clover Blossom pure and white,
    Sweet, I love you so!
Put up your fragrant lips to-night,
    Kiss me before I go! "

O for the foolish Clover-Head!
    Bee is only a rover;
He whispers the same to the blushing Rose
    As merrily he flies over;
O for the trusting Clover-Head!
    " Bee is my honest lover!
He has naught to say to the Roses red,
    All for the little Clover! "

Little White Clover-head is gone,
    Trusting and sweet and loving!
Over the fields the Bee alone,
    Humming an air goes roving!

DANDELION.

Young Dandelion, the miser,
  With pockets full of gold,
Had wooed the Violet royal,
  While yet the days were cold.
But Violet, fair maiden,
  Was far too sweet for him;
She faded with the May-time;
  Her tender eyes grew dim.

Sweet Violet had vanished;
  The Daisies only knew
The place where loving Fairies
  Had hid her eyes of blue.
O Dandelion! Poor laddie!
  In one short Summer night,
His hair so golden, golden,
  Had turned to silvery white!

He kissed no more the Sunbeams,
  Nor stored their yellow gold!
Sweet Violet was sleeping;
  Young Dandelion was old.
O blessings on the Fairies!
  They sent a wind one day
And bore the white-haired lover
  To Violet away!

27

SLEEPY-HEADS.

Rap! Rap! against the window
 Comes the thick-falling rain;
April is calling her children
 Back to her bosom again.
Loud blows the wind in his trumpet,
 Fiercely he shrieks in their ears!
"Come, Grasses, O dainty green Grasses,
 April is waiting in tears!

"Come Violet, modest wee blossom,
 O show us your bonny blue eyes!
Come, Columbine dear, and Arbutus:
 It is time for you all to arise!
Come, Dandelion, yellow-haired laddie,
 The Crocus is waiting for you!
She threw off her warm winter blanket,
 And so did the Daffodil too!"

The Posies they turned on their pillows,
 And lazily answered him, "Yes!"
Then sleepily looking about them,
 They said, "It is late we confess!
But we won't disappoint the sweet babies,
 We are coming up now with a bound!
When the children come calling upon us
 They will find us all out of the ground!"

HOLLY-HOCKS.

DOLLIES sweet in gardens grow!
  Shiny-eyes will tell you so!
Dainty maids in silken frocks
  Blossom on the holly-hocks!
Here's a lady clad in silk;
  There's another white as milk!
Bowing low at every breeze
  These are what my lassie sees!
Dainty maids in silken frocks,
  Blooming on the holly-hocks!

HEPATICA.

HEPATICA TRILOBA, wrapped all in furs,
    Sleeps all the day in that queer nest of hers.
Sleeps till the Sun steals her blanket away,
    Bravely she rises and blesses the day!
Wise little blossom! She keeps on her furs!
    A clear little head is that shy one of hers!
Sagely she says: " Though the Spring brings
      the Swallow,
    Snowflakes and Icicles surely will follow! "
Dear little blossom, thou darling of Spring,
    Cheery and bright is the message you bring!
Hepatica Triloba, gowned all in blue,
    I'm glad for the Springtime, and Sunlight
      and You!

A VALENTINE.

LIKE a blossom in the snow,
  In the snow a bloom of white.
Go, my little Cupid, go!
  Like a blossom in the snow!
With your arrow and your bow,
  And your eyes with love a-light!
Like a blossom in the snow,
  In the snow a bloom of white!

Tell my lady of my love,
  Of my love the long day through!
Fair is she as skies above—
  Tell my lady of my love!
Fly! with wing of carrier-dove,
  Greet my lady sweet and true:
Tell my lady of my love,
  Of my love the long day through!

ROBIN'S CHOICE.

The Maple shook her leaflets
    With a sweet and soothing sound,
And a shower of scarlet blossoms
    Fell thick upon the ground.
With a soft persuasive murmur
    She waved her arms and said,
"Come hither, Richard Robin,
    With your russet coat and red!
Within my shady branches
    There is quietude and rest!
Come hither, Richard Robin,
    And build your cozy nest!"

The Pine-tree looked and listened,
    And she sighed both sad and sweet;
For she had no graceful blossoms
    To fling at Robin's feet.
So she only waved her branches,
    And then sighing softly said:
"You hear her, Richard Robin,
    And you nod your russet head!
But I have nought to offer!
    And I can only weep!
But one thing, Richard Robin,
    I'll rock your babes to sleep!"

32

Dick Robin looked and listened,
    As he plumed his ruddy breast;
Before the week had ended,
    He had built his cozy nest.
There, half hidden in the branches,
    It is built full warm and deep;
And four little chirping Robins
    The Pine-tree rocks to sleep!

EASTER MORN.

EASTER lilies, fresh, new-born,
   Blossom for this holy morn.
Christ is risen!   Angels sing.
   " Glory be to God, our King!
Hail, ye mortals, hail the day
   Angels rolled the stone away! "

Bloom, Arbutus, fragrant, sweet!
   Lay your blossoms at His feet.
Bloom with rosy, sun-rise hues,
   Born of forest damps and dews!
Bloom, ye Wind-flower! Lift your head,
   Christ is risen from the dead!

CHILDHOOD MEMORIES.

I can see the brown old house,
    With its peach-tree by the door;
See the gnarled old apple boughs
    With their fruitage bending o'er;

See the hollyhocks and pinks,
    And the pansies' velvet eyes;
And my heart grows young, methinks,
    With an ever new surprise.

For I see within the door
    Grandpa with his beard of grey—
Grandma with her smile of yore,
    Ah! could I call back the day!

Never pair in years to be
    Read so well my heart's dear dreams;
Never faith so full and free
    In my wildest plans and schemes!

I can hear the sifting snow
    Beating on the window panes;
Hear the patter, soft and low,
    Of the gentle April rains.

35

See the orchard's gnarlèd trees—
  (Many a low and quiet nook,
Known alone to birds and bees,
  Covèrt dear for child and book!)

Here a blossom all unseen,
  Snugly hid from passers-by,
Nestled under leaves of green
  Learning secrets of the sky!

Dreamed her dreams and straight forgot;
  Learned the robin's cheerful song:
Revelled in her happy lot:
  Knew no trouble all day long.

Learned the language of the flowers:
  All the woodland secrets knew:
Nests that swung in leafy bowers:
  Where the earliest berries grew!

Long she rests whose willing ear
  Heard the story of the day!
Blessèd soul, who loved to hear
  All the childish lips would say!

Would my verse could show her face!
  Naught my feeble hand can paint
Save the spirit's gentle grace,
  Save the halo 'round the Saint!

A FUNNY PARTY.

Miss Robin Redbreast's Kettle-drum :
She hopes that all her friends will come.
From Four to Six P. M.——N. B.
Miss Golden Oriole pours the tea !

The little Sparrow in her nest
With careful touches plumed her breast.
The brown Thrush came, the shyest bird,
Who trembled at the lightest word!

The guests were gay ; but all along
The party waited for a song.
The Robin came with eager wing
And begged the Bobolinks to sing.

The low tones trembled in their throats ;
They could not sing without their notes!
The brown Thrush said, " Pray do not scold !
But O ! I really have a cold ! "

And so the party all took wing,
For not a single bird would sing !
A funny party all agree,
Where Golden Oriole poured the tea !

WHAT THE FLY THINKS.

A FLY went buzzing over my head;
　　　　Buzz-z!　Buzz-z!
And what do you think the little fly said?
　　　　Buzz-z!　Buzz-z!

I saw two babies as I flew by
Begin to quarrel and then to cry!
Pretty children, their Grandma thinks,
Calls them her " Rosy-posy pinks!"

What does it mean when the babies cry?
Isn't it better to be a fly?
Babies laugh though, coo and smile,
Shriek with laughter once in a while.

Wonder what creatures with two legs do!
I never could live with so very few!
How do they ever get about?
Wonder who pulled their other legs out!

There!　They're going!　How　queer they
　　　　crawl!
Funny world! said the fly on the wall!

A fly went buzzing over my head,
　　　　Buzz-z!　Buzz-z!
And these are the words the little fly said,
　　　　Buzz-z!　Buzz-z!

SONG OF THE LITTLE FISHER.

O, THE fish may swish as much as they wish,
  And the grasshopper hie him away,
But I think on the whole with a line and a pole
  That I will go fishing to-day—
  Yes, I will go fishing to-day!

O, the worm may squirm, but I will be firm,
  For the worm will be part of the play!
So I think on the whole with a line and a pole
  That I will go fishing to-day—
  Yes, I will go fishing to-day!

O, the trout may pout as they scuttle about:
  I will drop them a line if I may,
For I think on the whole with a hook and a pole
  That I will go fishing to-day—
  Yes, I will go fishing to-day!

O, the fish may swish as much as they wish,
  And the grasshopper hie him away.
But I think on the whole with a line and a pole
  That I will go fishing to-day—
  Yes, I will go fishing to-day!

A QUEER HUNT.

Yo ho! Tally ho!
  To the chase! to the chase we go!
For a sly little fox,
  All hid in the rocks,
To the chase! to the chase we go!

Yo ho! Tally ho!
  Over the hills we go!
And our lively trail
  Is the fox's tail;
To the chase! to the chase we go!

Yo ho! Tally ho!
  Over the fields we go!
Like a streak of light
  Goes the luckless wight,
Over the fields, O ho!

Yo ho! Tally ho!
  Over the brook we go!
On a load of hay
  Rides a farmer gray,
Over the bridge, O ho!

Yo ho!   Tally ho!
    Where is the fox?   O ho!
Not a sight, not a trail
    Of his bushy tail!
Where is the fox?   O ho!

Yo ho!   Tally ho!
    Where did the sly fox go?
O, he hid in the hay
    And he chuckled away,
Safe was his tail, O ho!

Yo ho!   Tally ho!
    Where did the farmer go?
O, he rode into town
    As the fox jumped down!
Sly little fox, O ho!

PRINCESS TINY-MITE.

Our little Princess Tiny-mite,
  She hates to go to bed at night;
And yet awake she can not keep,
  But will keep dropping off to sleep.
" I am not sleepy! don't you see?"
  Says Princess Tiny-mite to me.
Now do you think she does just right,
  Our little Princess Tiny-mite?

Our little Princess Tiny-mite,
  She does not like to be polite;
And yet the Princess plainly sees
  All dainty maids say, if you please!
Now do you think she does just right,
  Our little Princess Tiny-mite?

Our little Princess Tiny-mite,
  She likes to see her fingers white;
But yet she hates the water so,
  With grimy fingers she will go.
Now do you think she does just right,
  Our little Princess Tiny-mite?

Our little Princess Tiny-mite,
    Is very precious in our sight!
Some day we hope our maid will see
    How very queer she used to be!
O funny, dancing, darling sprite!
    Our little Princess Tiny-mite!

TO GRACE.

Dear little maid by the name of Grace,
With quaintly serious downcast face,
Reading with earnest and thoughtful look;
Happily lost in a story-book!
I wonder—some day—when she older grows—
She may be a writer—ah! who knows!
Stranger things has this strange world seen,
Dear little maid with the thoughtful mien!
To-day is enough if she does her best;
God, her teacher, will do the rest!

44

TO A LITTLE CHILD.

An angel smiled this happy morn;
That hour a little child was born.
With silken hair and starry eyes
A little wanderer from the skies!
A little spirit free from guile,
And oh! she had that angel's smile!

MARGUERITE.

Baby with silken hair,
  With winsome and wise little face,
What are you dreaming about?
  You think this a strange, strange place,
    Baby my own, my sweet,
    Fair little Marguerite?

Baby with sea-shell hands;
  Fair as rose-petals each!
Whence came your bonny eyes
  And your cheeks like the downy peach,
    Baby my own, my sweet,
    Fair little Marguerite?

Baby with starry eyes,
  Whence came your royal air?
Did you lose your way from the throne
  With your crown of the silken hair,
    Baby my own, my sweet,
    Fair little Marguerite?

GOD'S GIFTS.

Dear little Edith, darling pet!
Sweetest maiden I've dreamed of yet!
Eyes wide open, and curls of gold,
Such was Edith at four years old.
Thoughtful lassie with earnest eyes
Opening oft with a sweet surprise,
Saying the queerest things, I know,
Ever a baby said below!

Edith's pet was a staid old hen,
Rich in a fluffy brood just then.
Just the cunningest, funniest sight!
Ten downy balls, all yellow and white.
Little Edith was looking wise,
Watching the chickens with earnest eyes:
"Choc'late," she said, with a thoughtful nod,
"Did you know your chicks were a dift from
          Dod?"

Darling maiden, I see her now,
Just as she looked with that thoughtful brow:
"Whatever put that in your curly head?"
Looking down with a smile I said.

47

Edith looked up in a sweet surprise,
Opening wider her earnest eyes.
" Why, mamma, you said I was that to you,
And I thought the chickens were Dod's dift
        too!"

IN FROGLAND.

Have you heard of the country of Bogland,
  In the famous Kingdom of Frogland?
Where each plump mother frog
  On a water-soaked log
Rocks Johnny and Peter and Polly Wog?

At night in this country of Bogland,
  In this famous Kingdom of Frogland,
Have you heard the poor mother
  Scold Pete and his brother,
And the froggies in turn all scolding each other?

In this curious country of Bogland,
  In the famous Kingdom of Frogland,
Frogs are naughty, I fear,
  Each night of the year:
Just listen some evening and you will hear!

TWINS.

Frowns and grimaces, the funniest faces,
  Tears and laughter and sighs!
Blows and caresses, and rumpled up dresses,
  Kisses and lunches and cries!
Moods delightful, angelic, and spiteful,
  (Queer little bundles of sins!)
Comical haughtiness, lovable naughtiness,
  These are our four-year-old twins.

Dear little images, quarrels and scrimmages,
  Bruises and tumbles and shrieks!
Moods devotional, saintly, emotional,
  Queer little changeable freaks!
None so dear as these, half so queer as these,
  (Quaint little bundles of sins!)
Lovable sweetness, childhood's completeness,
  Dear little four-year-old twins!

TO MARGARET.

LEARNING TO DANCE.

DANCE, little maid! Childhood soon is over!
  Dance while the bobolink is swinging on
      the clover!
Light hearts are happy hearts! Little maid,
      be merry!
  Dance e'er the blossom-drift has fallen from
      the cherry!
Happy hearts are pure hearts! Yours with
      love is laden!
  Dance then! Be merry then! Happy
      little maiden!

PETER PECULIAR.

Peter Peculiar was rich as a Jew.
      Every one knew!
But he wore an old hat,
Ragged coat and all that,
But his fortune, O nobody knew!

Peter Peculiar was fond of his cat.
      (I know that!)
And what was so funny,
He left all his money
To Puss—in the crown of his hat!

Peter Peculiar said in his will,
      "My cat Bill
Shall still live in my house
And wage war on Sir Mouse,
With a servant to feed him, shall Bill."

A little maid-servant, and plenty of mice,
      (It was nice!)
With cheese to make fat
The said mice for said cat,
And gridirons to broil in a trice!

But Bill he grew thinner, and some folks suppose,
  (No one knows!)
That Bill was ill treated,
And Peter was cheated—
This is just how the old story goes:

'Twas the maid that grew fat,
  Not the cat,
For she ate up his cheese,
Tho' she swore on her knees
That she never, no never, did that!

And the ribbons she flaunted! O yes!
  You may guess
Bill's friends were indignant,
At acts so malignant:
So they went to the law for redress.

Peter Peculiar's own cat, faithful Bill,
  Thriveth still!
But the maiden is dead:
She was hung, it is said,
By her ribbons, on Mulberry Hill!

MALCOLM'S PRAYER.

KARL is only a doggie,
    Handsome and wise and good;
And Malcolm is only a laddie
    Just out of babyhood.

Last night the laddie was kneeling
    Bent low at Grandma's knee:
" Make Malcolm mind his Mamma!
    And Grandma—let me see—

God bless my Mamma and Papa,
    And Grandma and Baby "—then
The laddie's head bent lower,
    " Please God, bless Karl—Amen ! "

POUTY-LIPS AND LAUGHING-EYES.

Pouty-lips and Laughing-eyes,
Queerest pair beneath the skies!
One is like the summer sun,
Thunder-cloud the other one!
Sometimes when the sun looks through,
Oh! how charming are the two!
Pouty-lips and Laughing-eyes,
Queerest pair beneath the skies!

Laughing-eyes and Pouty-lips
Full of queerest pranks and quips!
One they are, though often two!
Who can solve this rhyme for you?
One has eyes like any star;
Just the same the other's are!
Pouty-lips and Laughing-eyes,
Dearest pair beneath the skies!

WHAT RODDY SAW.

Roddy stood at the window
  Watching the western sky:
The sun had sunk behind the hills,
  And clouds went sailing by.

The moon rose o'er the garden trees,
  A crescent clear and pale :
And Roddy cried, " O Mamma, come !
  I see God's finger-nail ! "

TWO GIRLS.

I know a wee girl,
    With a pout and a curl:
The funniest under the sun.
    She cries when it rains
    On the window panes,
She cries when the rain is done.

I know a wee girl
    With a smile and a curl;
The prettiest under the skies;
    She laughs when it pours,
    And is happy indoors,
With fun looking out of her eyes.

Now which of these girls
    With the golden curls
Is greater help to her mother?
    The girlie who cries
    At the cloudy skies,
Or the girlie who laughs, like the other?

THE POST-OFFICE.

Down at Grandpa's use ter be
The queerest thing you ever see!
Why just a post-office on a tree!
Honest, just a wooden box,
'Thout any hinges, bars or locks—
Just a box nailed on a tree,
Queerest thing you ever see!

Ev'ry day from far and near
All the neighbors gathered here.
(I went long of Grandpa dear.)
There'd be letters just a few.
(Once't I found one, Pa, from you!)
Ev'ry day from far and near
All the neighbors gathered here!

Once't I found—now guess the rest!
'Course you can't! Well, 'twas a nest
Close into the corner press't.
Just you think! And still the same
Every day the neighbors came.
There it stayed all self-confess't
Just a little blue-bird's nest!

58

Down at Grandpa's use ter be
The queerest thing you ever see!
Why just a post-office on a tree!
How do you s'pose our own would work
With just a little bird for clerk?
Down at Grandpa's use ter be
Just a box nailed on a tree!

JACKIE WONDERS.

I WONDER, wonder all the day,
I hear our thoughtful Jackie say:
I wonder if this 'lectric light
Would make our biddies lay by night;
I wonder why I can not crawl
Like buzzing flies upon the wall;
I wonder why I can't eat flowers
Just like that bossy-calf of ours;
I wonder, wonder, wonder whether
God always likes His kind of weather!

WISHING.

On, I wish a big, big wish!
  But what can wishing do?
I wish I were a sailor-man.
  To sail the ocean blue.

And I wish I were a soldier.
  With a really truly gun :
And I wish I were a hunter bold,
  To make the tigers run.

And I wish I were a circus clown :
  But, oh! when night comes on.
I'd rather be of all the world
  My mamma's little John!

THAT SINGULAR BOY.

I know a boy, the strangest boy,
   He never shouts nor stamps his feet ;
He never pulls the pussy's tail,
   His voice is ever low and sweet ;
The strangest boy in all the lands,
   And, oh! he loves to wash his hands.

I know a boy, the strangest boy,
   He does not like to skate or coast ;
And flying kite or playing ball,
   He can't tell which he hates the most.
Where dwells the boy? Oh! come and look!
   Within the pages of a book !

KATRINKA.

WHEN sweet Katrinka goes to sleep,
  The owls around the corner peep;
And little mice go creep, creep, creep!
  When sweet Katrinka goes to sleep.

When sweet Katrinka sheds a tear,
  The little lambkins gather near;
And all the sheep say dear, dear, dear!
  When sweet Katrinka sheds a tear.

When sweet Katrinka wakes from sleep,
  The limber fishes laugh and leap;
And little birds go cheep, cheep, cheep!
  When sweet Katrinka wakes from sleep.

When sweet Katrinka's tears are dry,
  Each jolly lambkin winks his eye;
And all the sheep say fie, fie, fie!
  When sweet Katrinka's tears are dry.

IN DREAMLAND.

Hither and yon, hither and yon,
Where is my blessed baby gone?

Over the mountains, vales, and streams,
Into the land of Pleasant Dreams.

What is the baby doing there,
Tiny fingers and golden hair?

Learning, learning from angel-books
The secret of sunny and loving looks.

Eyes are learning to shine, not weep,
From the sunny folk in the Land of Sleep.

Fingers are learning to gently press
Mother's cheek with a light caress.

Lips to smile, and the little feet
To walk alone on the Dreamland Street.

Hither and yon, hither and yon,
Dear little girlie, how long you're gone!

Lips are smiling; some angel nigh
Kissed my darling and said good-bye.

Lids are parting; she's coming back
By the Fast Express on the Dreamland track.

Back she comes by a special train;
Stop the cradle!   She's home again.

CRADLE SONG.

Hush-a-by, baby!   The Sandman is near;
  Soft o'er the threshold his footsteps I hear;
Hush-a-by!   Rock-a-by!   Mother will go
  Over the fields where the lily-buds blow.
Hush-a-by!   Rock-a-by!   Baby's asleep!
  Watch o'er our darling the fairies will keep.
Hush-a-by, baby!   The Sandman is near;
  Soft o'er the threshold his footsteps I hear.
    Hush!   Hush-a-by!

SLEEP, BABY, SLEEP.

R. B. 1897.

SLEEP, baby, with the shining eyes,
Thou little guest from Paradise.
A dainty lad whose winning face
In all our hearts found tender place.
Sweet be thy sleep, O child at rest,
Soft-cradled on thy Father's breast.
An angel sent in mortal's guise,
To show the way to Paradise.
    Sleep, baby, sleep!

THE KISSIMEE RIVER.

WHEN the Sandman comes and I say good-
    night,
  I kiss my Mamma and hug her tight;
And then this rune to a slumberous tune,
  My darling Mamma will softly croon:
" Oh, we live on the Kissimee River,
  Where the sunlight and shade are a-quiver;
And I kiss you Good-night as I hold you tight,
  Afloat on the Kissimee River.
Oh, the soft-flowing Kissimee River!"

When the Sandman comes with his Dreamland
    sheep,
  I kiss my Mamma and fall asleep;
To the gentle rune of a slumberous tune
  My darling Mamma will softly croon:
" Oh, we live on the Kissimee River,
  Where the sunlight and shade are a-quiver;
And I kiss you Good-night as I hold you tight,
  Afloat on the Kissimee River,
Oh, the soft-flowing Kissimee River!"

TO A CHILD.

FAIR are the lilies of the field,
    And sweet the wayside rose.
But fairer is my darling girl
    Than any flower that blows;
And brighter are her darling eyes
    Than any gem beneath the skies.

BABY ELAINE.

Dear little Baby Elaine,
  With winsome and wise little air;
Where did you come from, dear,
  Crowned with the silken hair,
      Baby Elaine?

Dear little Baby Elaine,
  Out of the heart of a flower,
A sweet little wandering fay,
  Queen of a happy hour,
      Baby Elaine.

Dear little Baby Elaine,
  So loving, tender, and sweet,
Are you one of the thoughts of God,
  Sent here to guide our feet,
      Baby Elaine?

Dear little Baby Elaine,
  Welcome whenever you come,
Golden-aureoled queen,
  Over our happy home,
      Baby Elaine!

A JINGLE.

As I was going to Kalamazoo,
　　　Kalamazoo Mazindy!
Oh, I met a Cat and a Kitten or two,
　　　Kalamazoo Mazindy!
"Oh! Madam Felicia," I said, said I,
　　　Kalamazoo Mazindy,
"I saw three mice in a lane hard by,"
　　　Kalamazoo Mazindy!
Now what came next, oh! never I knew,
　　　Kalamazoo Mazindy!
Away went a Cat and a Kitten or two,
　　　Kalamazoo Mazindy.
But I think that they dined on a mouse-ragout,
　　　Kalamazoo Mazindy!

INDIAN LULLABY.

Swing, swing, little boy, swing!
Lullabies soft shall the little birds sing,
Soon will the sun go to sleep in the West,
Sleep, little boy, like a bird in its nest!
Swing, swing! Breezes shall blow,
Hush! for thy mother is watching below.

DEPRIVATION.

I SING a song of the little child,
　The waif of the turbulent street :
The desolate child who patters the bricks,
　With bare and brown little feet.

I sing a song of the little child—
　The child who never an hour
Has roamed the meadow or watched the birds,
　Or held in her fingers a flower.
The child who never has seen, alas !
The green, green sky of the flower-starred grass.

Alas for the eyes that never have seen
The skies grow blue and the fields grow green !

73

TO MARJORIE.

I know a castle—built of love, no more—
　　Whose royal queen is just a baby girl!
Her throne, a rug upon the nursery floor;
　　Her sweet head's crown, full many a silken
　　　　curl.

Herein are subjects to her royal will,
If she would sleep, then all the house grows still!
If she be sad, her subjects all fall down;
Sad with her sadness; frowning if she frown.
Love is her sceptre; by its cunning art
Her chiefest captive is her mother's heart.

I know a castle—built of love, no more—
　　Whose royal queen is just a baby girl.
Her throne, a rug upon the nursery floor;
　　Her sweet head's crown, full many a silken
　　　　curl!

A LEGEND OF THE ROBIN.

THERE is a legend—sweet, the story runs—
   How a little bird came down,
And strove on the cruel cross to pluck
   The thorns from the Savior's crown:
How it plucked and plucked with its little beak
   Till its strength was well-nigh spent,
And over its breast, by the thorns deep-pierced,
   Its own blood coursing went.
And the Savior opened His weary eyes,
   And he said: "O brave little heart,
Thou hast eased a pang of my suffering
   And acted a blessed part;
Henceforward, ruddy thy breast shall be,
   O brave little sprite of the air,
And the loving heart of a little bird
   Shall rest in My sheltering care.

THE PARISH CHAISE.

In days of old
The tale is told.
Good Master Hallowell's English gold,
With good intention,
A rare invention
Bought of the owner, who marked it sold
(A bit for the buyer as well, I hold).

Wheels it had, and a lumbering seat.
Hood overhead and a floor for feet ;
As an antique wonder it couldn't be beat.
The people flew to the doors to spy
What Thing of Satan was tearing by :
The children hid in their mother's gown
When this strange apparition appeared in
        town :
Each dog went fleeing with folded tail,
Till the very milk in the pans turned pale :
But on it rolled till it seemed a speck,
And the gallant driver was still on deck.

But little by little the people found
No way like this to cover the ground ;

78

And the parson came with his hat in his hands,
Slick and shining from boots to bands,
                    Begging to borrow
                    The chaise to-morrow,
To see his parish and soothe their sorrow.
And Robert of Hallowell bowed his head,
" Take it and welcome, sir," he said !

And the carpenter came with his hammer and
        rule,
And the pedagogue grim on his way to the
        school.
And Robert of Hallowell every day
Spake like the Quaker, and answered, " Yea !"
And the blacksmith came, and he begged a ride
To Mooselookmeguntic to bring him a bride.
                    And the lawyer big,
                    With his powdered wig,
Butcher and baker borrowed the rig.

The farmer's dame she drove into town
To buy her daughter a linsey gown ;
No soul in the parish far and wide,
But came to His Honor and begged a ride.
And Robert of Hallowell said, said he,
" 'Tis plain this invention is not for me ;
                    For when I would roam
                    It is never at home,
But abroad in the parish its tracks I see."

'Tis a hundred years, or 'tis thereabout,
Since this public conveyance at last gave out :
    But there's lasting praise
    For the olden days,
And a rollicking cheer for the Parish Chaise.

———

1789 or 1790. " The first wheel carriage was a venerable chaise already outlawed by fashion in Boston, brought here by Mr. Hallowell. It was one of the first chaises invented, and was called by the owner ' the Parish Chaise,' for the appropriate reason that the whole parish borrowed it."—*History of Gardiner, Maine, p. 164.*

ALONE.

She lived alone; no other friend
  To cheer her or to bless;
Alone with one wee laughing boy
  To cherish and caress.

She lived apart; and no one knew
  Her history or name;
And no one strove to seek her out;
  Alone she went and came.

The little child, she loved him so!
  Bright was his shining hair;
His little presence seemed to make
  A glory everywhere.

His little face, one heavenly smile,
  It always seemed to say:
"God sent me down to lead you home
  His straight and narrow way."

The days went on. She went and came.
  The shadows on her face;
And still the little fair-haired boy
  Made bright the darkest place.

And summer passed, and winter came
   The snows fell thick and fast :
And still, upon the coldest days,
   We watched them hurrying past.

We saw her face grow white and thin.
   One day she was alone.
We saw how sad her weary eyes,
   How gray her hair had grown.

Day followed day. She went and came :
   No angel at her side.
We took no heed, but deeper plunged
   In selfishness and pride.

The winter passed. The snow-drop came ;
   The crocus reared its head.
She passed no longer day by day.
   The bright-haired boy was dead.

She was alone. Outside her door
   The spring birds carolled sweet :
And springing grass and violets
   Rose up to kiss her feet.

She did not see. Her eyes were dim.
   With tears were brimming o'er ;
She only saw the bit of crape
   That floated at the door.

And no one came to comfort her:
　　The child was all she had;
No more his laughter greeted her,
　　Nor prattle made her glad.

Alone and comfortless she dwelt;
　　Flowers bloomed around her door;
The robin strove to comfort her
　　With music welling o'er.

The very blossoms seemed to love
　　Her sweet and shadowed face;
They clustered 'round her cottage door,
　　And perfumed all the place.

They loved her all. 'Twas God who spoke
　　In birds and buds and flowers;
But earth-born children had no word
　　To cheer her lonely hours.

And so she lived and so she died,
　　Unknown until the last;
Back to her Savior and her boy
　　Her ransomed spirit passed.

Oh, shame! that such a thing could be
　　'Mid homes of wealth and fame;
That still through all her weary life
　　Alone she went and came.

A MODERN SAINT.

COME, sit on my knee, little Alice.
    A story? And what shall it be?
" Of a saint—and of one that was truly
    A plain little maiden like me! "

Ah! sweet little, grave little Alice,
    I would I could paint for your eyes
The soul of a maiden who truly
    Is one of God's saints in disguise.

You thought them all dead, little Alice?
    No nimbus of glory they wear;
God's sunshine gleams out of their faces,
    And this is the glory they bear!

Come, nestle your head on my shoulder.
    There once was a maiden like you,
Whose heart was kept eagerly seeking
    For some special mission to do.

Some great work this little maid asked for;
    Yet bravely she went on her way,
And did all the work that the Master
    Had happened to place in her way.

There were tired little children to comfort,
  And bruised little fingers to dress:
And never a child was too naughty
  To cuddle and soothe and caress.

And yet all the while she was asking:
  " Now how can a maiden like me
Best please the dear Jesu and Mary,
  Who held that sweet Child on her knee?"

And ever she looked for the answer,
  And longed for some mission to do.
I think, all the while, little Alice,
  She was doing God's mission, don't you?

It was: "Give me some great work, O Master,
  To die, it may be, for my King;
To write some great song, full of service,
  That armies and nations shall sing!

Yet ever her heart made its music;
  For others the guerdon might be.
Yet never a helmeted maiden
  Could better do battle than she.

And so all the days of her lifetime
  She spends, all unknowing her worth;
As truly a saint as the purest
  That ever was known upon earth.

Ah! maidens may go on their missions,
  But even a wee one, like you,
Need never go sighing and seeking
  For work of the Master's to do.

Be firm, little feet, for the service:
  Be strong, little hands, for the fray.
And the smallest of maidens, like Alice,
  May win to a saintship some day.

CETOBRIGA.

O RUINED town beneath the wave,
      Cetobriga!   Cetobriga!
Church, manse, and tower, how strange a grave,
      Cetobriga!   Cetobriga!

Thy buried streets a restless throng
Long ages past has swept along;
Thy walls have stirred to shout and song,
      Cetobriga!   Cetobriga!

The startled fisher sees to-day,
      Cetobriga!   Cetobriga!
Thy gleaming towers beneath the bay,
      Cetobriga!   Cetobriga!

Strange trick of Fate, that none should know
What dire disaster laid thee low,
Still through thy streets the salt waves flow,
      Cetobriga!   Cetobriga!

AN OLD-TIME LEGEND.

SWEET is the legend of that old-time day,
When fair Boy Jesus modeled birds in clay;
And all the lads, with shouts of boyish glee.
Came flocking near, the little birds to see.
Beneath His fingers wondrously they grew;
Soft breathed He on them, and afar they flew,
O wondrous story! So I think some day
The dear Lord will give wings to us, His clay.

WHEN AGNES LAUGHS.

WHEN Agnes laughs
  I hear the summer rains
Come tinkle tankle
  On the window panes.

I hear the brook go dancing on its way,
Mad with the music of an April day,
As tinkle tankle o'er the stones it slips,
Like the soft laughter from our Agnes' lips.
All this I hear.   The music of the woods,
The laugh of nature in her sunniest moods,
        When Agnes laughs.

THE MAIDEN'S SONG.

The King sent forth a message. There it said:
"Who sweetest sings before me, I will wed."
Mahalath heard the words. She knew no song,
But only served her Master all day long:
But in her heart she said: "My Lord and King,
I can but hear the songs the others sing."
So onward to the palace one bright day.
With heart of cheer, Mahalath sped her way.

Her lissome tread scarce bent the feathered grass.
The flowers peeped forth to see the maiden pass.
Onward she went. The road had rougher
     grown.
Her heart sang. "Wait. It leadeth to a
     throne."
Fair girls trooped by her. Though the path
     was wide.
Each from the little maiden turned aside.
Mahalath noted: "What am I to care?
A maid who waits behind her Master's chair!"

The sunlight kissed the maiden's golden head.
"Sing, happy heart," the little sparrows said.

Sharp were the stones that tore her little feet.
But still her heart sang. "Wait, the end is
    sweet."
She heard a moan, and close beside the way
An aged man, all worn and bleeding, lay.
The maid stood still.   Her gentle heart made
    moan.
" Oh, what are all the songs before the throne?

Here's work to do straight from the Master's
    hand.
My father sees me ; He will understand."
She dipped her kerchief in the running brook
And bathed his wounds with many a pitying
    look ;
Then raised the stranger to his trembling feet,
And soothed his terror with her accents sweet.
Onward they went.   The maiden's heart was
    light :
Fair in the distance shone the palace bright.

The way was long ; the old man feebler grown ;
And oft they rested by some wayside stone :
Then on once more, and still the maiden's
    song :
" O sweet the end, although the way is long."
The goal was reached.   " Haste, haste ! " the
    warder cried.
Creak went the hinges, and the gate swung
    wide.

She entered in.   Alone she went her way;
Her burden vanished like the light of day.

Next morn the palace thronged with happy
        guests;
Song after song fulfilled the King's behests.
Mahalath's heart was glad; behind the crowd
She clapped her hands and gaily laughed
        aloud.
Happy in other's joy, her simple heart
In jealous envy found no bitter part.

The songs were done.   The King stepped
        from his throne
To where the sweet Mahalath stood alone.
He took her hand : " Here stands a little maid
To do an act of kindness unafraid;
Good people, know, she helped me on my way,
Her singing heart made glad the fading day.
Be this my Queen.   Haste, little trembling
        feet;
Though long the way, the end is very sweet."

JULY.

THE air is still. A yellow haze
   Steals slowly o'er the sky;
The roadside grass is dry and brown;
   The cows go lagging by;
And scarce the grasses seem to stir;
No sound beside the cricket's whirr.

The air is still. The dusty steeds
   Go slowly homeward for the night;
And one by one in village homes
   Shines forth the cheery evening light.
But hark, that piping noise again!
The robin redbreast calls for rain.

FATHERHOOD.

My little lad is scarce four summers old:
  He looks into my face and trusts in me.
So looking in Thy face, O Father mine,
  Shall I not trust in Thee?
        Hear, Merciful and Mild,
        I am Thy child.

My little lad has oft-times gone astray:
  Done things forbid, yet unafraid
Has sought my breast. And shall I not seek
    Thine,
  Though I have often sinned and disobeyed?
        Hear, O Thou Blameless One,
        I am Thy son!
        For looking in Thy face,
I read my pardon, see my sin aright,
        And seek Thy grace.

For so my little lad clings to my breast:
Sure there of refuge, he forgets the rest:
        So I to Thee,
        O Merciful and Mild,
        I am Thy child.

94

THE BIRD AND THE WIRES.

'Twas a cold, little sparrow came my way,
    Sing hey! sing ho! little bird.
And what goes on in the world, I pray?
    "Speak low, O low," said the bird.
"O I sit on the wires, and under my feet
Go words of sorrow, O sad! O sweet!"
    Speak soft, speak low, little bird.

Now tell me the words that the strange wires
        say,
O sweet, O cold little stray:
"Says one: 'Our mother is lying dead.'
Another: 'Our Julia to-day is wed.'
And again: 'Rejoice, for a son is born.'
And another: 'I only am left forlorn.'
And the wires they tremble beneath my feet
And over and over the words repeat.
For 'tis now a smile, and 'tis now a sigh
That under my feet goes hurrying by.
'Tis a queer old world I have often heard.
Sing hey! sing ho!" said the wise little bird.

RING, CHRISTMAS BELLS.

RING, merry bells, on Christmas Day!
    Ring, bells, ring!
Good-will on earth your clangings say!
    Ring, bells, ring!
Ring out your message, sweet and clear,
This happiest day of all the year.
    Ring, bells, ring!

Ring, merry bells, across the snow!
    Ring, bells, ring!
Ring loud and sweet, ring soft and low.
    Ring, bells, ring!
Ring out your best, for on this morn
Across the sea our Lord was born.
    Ring, bells, ring!

Ring, merry bells, on Christmas Day!
    Ring, bells, ring!
Good-will on earth your clangings say.
    Ring, bells, ring!
Ring out your message, sweet and clear,
This happiest day of all the year.
    Ring, bells, ring!

www.ingramcontent.com/pod-product-compliance
Lightning Source LLC
Chambersburg PA
CBHW022012050726
47499CB00007BA/2407